Index

airplane 11
bike 8, 9
bus 6
rocket 12
train 10
walk 4

About the Author

Lori Mortensen lives in Northern California with her family and her cat, Max. When she's not tapping away at her computer, she's getting from here to there all sorts of ways. Her favorite is going on a long walk just before sunrise. Trains are nice too.

© 2019 Rourke Educational Media

All rights reserved. No part of this book may be reproduced or utilized in any form or by any means, electronic or mechanical including photocopying, recording, or by any information storage and retrieval system without permission in writing from the publisher.

www.rourkeeducationalmedia.com

PHOTO CREDITS: Cover ©franckreporter, ©jacktheflipper, Page 3 ©aldomurillo, Page 4-5 ©By BYUNGSUK KO, Page 2,6,14,15 ©Tholer, Page 7 ©IPGGutenbergUKLtd, Page 2,8-9,14,15 ©monkeybusinessimages, Page 2,10,14,15 ©LeoPatrizi, Page 11 ©sharply_done, Page 2,12,14,15 ©nasa.gov, Page 13, ©lmgorthand

Edited by: Keli Sipperley
Cover design by: Kathy Walsh
Interior design by: Kathy Walsh

Library of Congress PCN Data
Transportation / Lori Mortensen
(Let's Find Out)
ISBN (hard cover)(alk. paper) 978-1-64156-195-2
ISBN (soft cover) 978-1-64156-251-5
ISBN (e-Book) 978-1-64156-301-7
Library of Congress Control Number: 2017957805

Printed in the United States of America, North Mankato, Minnesota

Photo Glossary

 **bike** (bike): A bicycle, motorcycle, or motorbike.

 **bus** (buhs): A large vehicle that can carry many people.

 **rocket** (RAH-kit): A tube-shaped vehicle with a powerful engine that travels through space.

 **train** (trayn): A group of railroad cars that are connected to each other and travel on a railway.

Did you find these words?

Sometimes, a **bike** gets you there.

If it's too far, some people ride the **bus**.

Sometimes a **rocket** is the only way.

Some people take the **train**.

How do you get from here to there?

Sometimes a **rocket** is the only way.

Or an airplane.

Some people take the **train**.

train

Sometimes a **bike** gets you there.

Or drive a car.

If it's too far, some people ride the **bus**.

bus

People walk if it's not too far.

Transportation

How do you get from here to there?

Can you find these words?

bike

bus

rocket

train

Table of Contents

Transportation   3

Photo Glossary   15

Index   16

About the Author   16

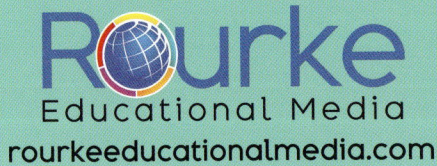